PUFFIN BOOKS

The Sheep-Pig

Dick King-Smith served in the Grenadier Guards during the Second World War, and afterwards spent twenty years as a farmer in Gloucestershire, the county of his birth. Many of his stories are inspired by his farming experiences. Later he taught at a village primary school. His first book, *The Fox Busters*, was published in 1978. Since then he has written a great number of children's books, including *The Sheep-Pig* (winner of the Guardian Award and filmed as *Babe*), *Harry's Mad*, *Noah's Brother*, *The Hodgeheg*, *Martin's Mice*, *Ace*, *The Cuckoo Child* and *Harriet's Hare* (winner of the Children's Book Award in 1995). At the British Book Awards in 1991 he was voted Children's Author of the Year. He has three children, a large number of grandchildren and several great-grandchildren, and lives in a seventeenth-century cottage only a crow's-flight from the house where he was born.

Dick King-Smith
The Sheep-Pig

Illustrated by Ann Kronheimer

PUFFIN BOOKS

PUFFIN BOOKS

Published by the Penguin Group
Penguin Books Ltd, 80 Strand, London WC2R 0RL, England
Penguin Putnam Inc., 375 Hudson Street, New York, New York 10014, USA
Penguin Books Australia Ltd, 250 Camberwell Road, Camberwell, Victoria 3124, Australia
Penguin Books Canada Ltd, 10 Alcorn Avenue, Toronto, Ontario, Canada M4V 3B2
Penguin Books India (P) Ltd, 11 Community Centre, Panchsheel Park, New Delhi – 110 017, India
Penguin Books (NZ) Ltd, Cnr Rosedale and Airborne Roads, Albany, Auckland, New Zealand
Penguin Books (South Africa) (Pty) Ltd, 24 Sturdee Avenue, Rosebank 2196, South Africa

Penguin Books Ltd, Registered Offices: 80 Strand, London WC2R 0RL, England

www.penguin.com

First published by Victor Gollancz 1983
Published in Puffin Books 1985
Published in this edition 2003
14

Text copyright © Fox Busters Ltd, 1983
Illustrations copyright © Ann Kronheimer, 2003
All rights reserved

The moral right of the author and illustrator has been asserted

Set in 15/18.5 Perpetua

Made and printed in England by Clays Ltd, St Ives plc

Except in the United States of America, this book is sold subject to the condition that it shall not, by way of
trade or otherwise, be lent, re-sold, hired out, or otherwise circulated without the publisher's prior consent in
any form of binding or cover other than that in which it is published and without a similar condition including
this condition being imposed on the subsequent purchaser

British Library Cataloguing in Publication Data
A CIP catalogue record for this book is available from the British Library

ISBN 0–141–31600–4

Contents

One
'Guess My Weight'

'What's that noise?' said Mrs Hogget, sticking her comfortable round red face out of the kitchen window. 'Listen, there 'tis again, did you hear it, what a racket, what a row, anybody'd think someone was being murdered, oh dearie me, whatever is it, just listen to it, will you?'

Farmer Hogget listened. From the usually quiet valley below the farm came a medley of sounds: the oompah oompah of a brass band, the shouts of children, the rattle and thump of a skittle alley, and every now and then a very high, very loud, very angry-sounding squealing lasting perhaps ten seconds.

Farmer Hogget pulled out an old pocket-watch as big round as a saucer and looked at it. 'Fair starts at two,' he said. 'It's started.'

'I knows that,' said Mrs Hogget, 'because I'm late now with all theseyer cakes and jams and pickles and preserves as is meant to be on the Produce Stall this very minute, and who's going to take them there, I'd like to know, why you are, but afore you does, what's that noise?'

The squealing sounded again.

'That noise?'

Mrs Hogget nodded a great many times. Everything that she did was done at great length, whether it was speaking or simply nodding her head. Farmer Hogget, on the other hand, never wasted his energies or his words.

'Pig,' he said.

Mrs Hogget nodded a lot more.

'I thought 'twas a pig, I said to meself that's a

pig that is, only nobody round here do keep pigs, 'tis all sheep for miles about, what's a pig doing, I said to meself, anybody'd think they was killing the poor thing, have a look when you take all this stuff down, which you better do now, come and give us a hand, it can go in the back of the Land Rover, 'tisn't raining, 'twon't hurt, wipe your boots afore you comes in.'

'Yes,' said Farmer Hogget.

When he had driven down to the village and made his delivery to the Produce Stall, Farmer Hogget walked across the green, past the Hoopla Stall and the Coconut Shy and the Aunt Sally and the skittles and the band, to the source of the squealing noise, which came every now and again from a small pen of hurdles in a far corner, against the churchyard wall.

By the pen sat the Vicar, notebook in hand, a cardboard box on the table in front of him. On the hurdles hung a notice – 'Guess my weight. Ten pence a go.' Inside was a little pig.

As Farmer Hogget watched, a man leaned over and picked it out of the pen. He hefted it in both hands, frowning and pursing his lips in a considering way, while all the time the piglet struggled madly and yelled blue murder. The moment it was put down, it quietened. Its eyes, bright intelligent eyes, met the farmer's. They regarded one another.

One saw a tall thin brown-faced man with very long legs, and the other saw a small fat pinky-white animal with very short ones.

'Ah, come along, Mr Hogget!' said the Vicar. 'You never know, he could be yours for ten pence. Guess his weight correctly, and at the end of the day you could be taking him home!'

'Don't keep pigs,' said Farmer Hogget. He stretched out a long arm and scratched its back. Gently, he picked it up and held it before his face. It stayed quite still and made no sound.

'That's funny,' said the Vicar. 'Every time so far that someone has picked him up he's screamed his head off. He seems to like you. You'll have to have a guess.'

Carefully, Farmer Hogget put the piglet back in the pen. Carefully, he took a ten pence piece from his pocket and dropped it in the cardboard box. Carefully, he ran one finger down the list of guesses already in the Vicar's notebook.

'Quite a variation,' said the Vicar. 'Anything from twenty pounds to forty, so far.' He wrote down 'Mr Hogget' and waited, pencil poised.

Once again, slowly, thoughtfully, the farmer picked the

piglet up.

Once again, it remained still and silent.

'Thirty-one pounds,' said Farmer Hogget. He put the little pig down again. 'And a quarter,' he said.

'Thirty-one and a quarter pounds. Thank you, Mr Hogget. We shall be weighing the little chap at about half past four.'

'Be gone by then.'

'Ah well, we can always telephone you. If you should be lucky enough to win him.'

'Never win nothing.'

As he walked back across the green, the sound of the pig's yelling rang out as someone else had a go.

'You do never win nothing,' said Mrs Hogget at tea-time, when her husband, in a very few words, had explained matters, 'though I've often thought I'd like a pig, we could feed un on scraps, he'd come just right for Christmas time, just think, two nice hams, two sides of bacon, pork chops, kidneys, liver, chitterling, trotters, save his blood for black pudding, there's the phone.'

Farmer Hogget picked it up.

'Oh,' he said.

Two
'There. Is That Nice?'

In the farmyard, Fly the black and white collie was beginning the training of her four puppies. For some time now they had shown an instinctive interest in anything that moved, driving it away or bringing it back, turning it to left or right, in fact herding it. They had begun with such things as passing beetles, but were now ready, Fly considered, for larger creatures.

She set them to work on Mrs Hogget's ducks.

Already the puppies were beginning to move as

sheep-dogs do, seeming to creep rather than walk, heads held low, ears pricked, eyes fixed on the angrily quacking birds as they manoeuvred them about the yard.

'Good boys,' said Fly. 'Leave them now. Here comes the boss.'

The ducks went grumbling off to the pond, and the five dogs watched as Farmer Hogget got out of the Land Rover.

He lifted something out of a crate in the back, and carried it into the stables.

'What was that, Mum?' said one of the puppies.

'That was a pig.'

'What will the boss do with it?'

'Eat it,' said Fly, 'when it's big enough.'

'Will he eat us,' said another rather nervously, 'when we're big enough?'

'Bless you,' said his mother. 'People only eat stupid animals. Like sheep and cows and ducks and chickens. They don't eat clever ones like dogs.'

'So pigs are stupid?' said the puppies.

Fly hesitated. On the one hand, having been born and brought up in sheep country, she had in fact never been personally acquainted with a pig. On the other, like most mothers, she did not wish to appear ignorant before her children.

'Yes,' she said. 'They're stupid.'

At this point there came from the kitchen window a long burst of words like the rattle of a machine-gun, answered by a single shot from the stables, and Farmer Hogget emerged and crossed the yard towards the farmhouse with his loping stride.

'Come on,' said the collie bitch. 'I'll show you.'

The floor of the stables had not rung to a horse's hoof for many years, but it was a useful place for storing things. The hens foraged about there, and sometimes laid their eggs in the old wooden mangers; the swallows built their nests against its roof-beams with mud from the duckpond; and rats and mice lived happy lives in its shelter until the farm cats cut them short. At one end of the stables were two loose-boxes with boarded sides topped by iron rails. One served as a kennel for Fly and her puppies. The other sometimes housed sick sheep. Here Farmer Hogget had shut the piglet.

A convenient stack of straw bales allowed the dogs to look down into the box through the bars.

'It certainly looks stupid,' said one of the puppies, yawning. At the sound of the words the piglet glanced up quickly. He put his head on one side and regarded the dogs with sharp eyes. Something about the sight of this very small

animal standing all by itself in the middle of the
roomy loose-box touched Fly's soft heart.
Already she was sorry that she had said that pigs
were stupid, for this one certainly did not appear
to be so. Also there was something dignified
about the way it stood its ground, in a strange
place, confronted with strange animals. How
different from the silly sheep, who at the mere
sight of a dog would run aimlessly about, crying

'Wolf! Wolf!' in their empty-headed way.

'Hullo,' she said. 'Who are you?'

'I'm a Large White,' said the piglet.

'Blimey!' said one of the puppies. 'If that's a large white, what's a small one like?' And they all four sniggered.

'Be quiet!' snapped Fly. 'Just remember that five minutes ago you didn't even know what a pig was.' And to the piglet she said kindly, 'I expect that's your breed, dear. I meant, what's your name?'

'I don't know,' said the piglet.

'Well, what did your mother call you, to tell you apart from your brothers and sisters?' said

Fly and then wished she hadn't, for at the mention of his family the piglet began to look distinctly unhappy. His little forehead wrinkled and he gulped and his voice trembled as he answered.

'She called us all the same.'

'And what was that, dear?'

'Babe,' said the piglet, and the puppies began to giggle until their mother silenced them with a growl.

'But that's a lovely name,' she said. 'Would you like us to call you that? It'll make you feel more at home.'

At this last word the little pig's face fell even further.

'I want my mum,' he said very quietly.

At that instant the collie bitch made up her mind that she would foster this unhappy child.

'Go out into the yard and play,' she said to the puppies, and she climbed to the top of the straw stack and jumped over the rail and down into the loose-box beside the piglet.

'Listen, Babe,' she said. 'You've got to be a brave boy. Everyone has to leave their mother, it's all part of growing up. I did so, when I was your age, and my puppies will have to leave me quite soon. But I'll look after you. If you like.' Then she licked his little snout with a warm rough tongue, her plumed tail wagging.

'There. Is that nice?' she said.

A little while later, Farmer Hogget came into the stables with his wife, to show her his prize. They looked over the loose-box door and saw, to their astonishment, Fly curled round the piglet. Exhausted by the drama of the day, he lay fast asleep against his new-found foster-parent.

'Well, will you look at that!' said Mrs Hogget. 'That old Fly, she'll mother anything, kittens, ducklings, baby chicks, she's looked after all of they, now 'tis a pig, in't he lovely, what a picture, good job he don't know where he'll finish up, but he'll be big then and we'll be glad to see the back of him, or the hams of him, I should say,

shan't us, wonder how I shall get it all in the freezer?'

'Pity. Really,' said Farmer Hogget absently.

Mrs Hogget went back to her kitchen, shaking her head all the way across the yard at the thought of her husband's soft-heartedness.

The farmer opened the loose-box door, and to save the effort of a word, clicked his fingers to call the bitch out.

As soon as Fly moved the piglet woke and

followed her, sticking so close to her that his snout touched her tail-tip. Surprise forced Farmer Hogget into speech.

'Fly!' he said in amazement. Obediently, as always, the collie bitch turned and trotted back to him. The pig trotted behind her.

'Sit!' said Farmer Hogget. Fly sat. Babe sat. Farmer Hogget scratched his head. He could not think of anything to say.

Three
'Why Can't I Learn?'

By dark it was plain to Farmer Hogget that, whether he liked it or no, Fly had not four, but five children.

All the long summer evening Babe had followed Fly about the yard and buildings, aimlessly, it seemed to the watching farmer, though of course this was not the case. It was in fact a conducted tour. Fly knew that if this foster-child was to be allowed his freedom and the constant reassurance of her company for which he obviously craved, he must quickly learn (and patently he was a quick learner) his way about the place; and that he must be taught, as her puppies had been taught, how to behave like a good dog.

'A pig you may be, Babe,' she had begun by saying, 'but if you do as I tell you, I shouldn't be a bit surprised if the boss doesn't let you run about with us, instead of shutting you up. He's a kind man, the boss is.'

'I knew that,' said Babe, 'when he first picked me up. I could feel it. I knew he wouldn't hurt me.'

'You wait . . .' began one of the puppies, and then stopped suddenly at his mother's warning growl. Though she said nothing, all four of her children knew immediately by instinct what she meant.

'Wait for what?' said Babe.

'Er . . . you wait half a tick, and we'll take you round and show you everything,' said the first puppy hastily. 'Won't we, Mum?'

So Babe was shown all round the yard and the farm buildings, and introduced to the creatures who lived thereabouts, the ducks and chickens and other poultry, and the farm cats. He saw no sheep, for they were all in the fields.

Even in the first hour he learned a number of useful lessons, as the puppies had learned before him: that cats scratch and hens peck, that turning your back on the turkey-cock means getting your bottom bitten, that chicks are not for chasing and eggs are not for eating.

'You do as I do,' said Fly, 'and you'll be all right.'

She thought for a moment. 'There is one thing though, Babe,' she said, and she looked across at the back door of the farmhouse, 'if I go in there, you stay outside and wait for me, understand?'

'Aren't pigs allowed in there?' asked Babe.

'Not live ones,' said one of the puppies, but he said it under his breath.

'No, dear,' said Fly. Well, not yet anyway, she thought, but the way you're going on, I shouldn't be surprised at anything. Funny, she thought, I feel really proud of him, he learns so quick. Quick as any sheep-dog.

That night the loose-box in which Babe had first been put was empty. In the next-door one, all six animals slept in the straw together. Though he did not tell his wife, Farmer Hogget had not had the heart to shut the piglet away, so happy was it in the company of the dogs.

At first the puppies had not been equally happy at the idea.

'Mum!' they said. 'He'll wet the bed!'

'Nonsense,' said Fly. 'If you want to do anything, dear, you go outside, there's a good boy.'

I nearly said 'there's a good pup' she thought. Whatever next!

In fact, in the days that followed, Babe became so doglike, what with coming when Fly came and sitting when Fly sat and much preferring dog's food to anything else he was offered, that Farmer Hogget caught himself half expecting, when he patted the piglet, that it would wag its tail. He would not have been surprised if it had tried to accompany Fly when he called her to go with him on his morning rounds, but it had stayed in the stables, playing with the puppies.

'You stop with the boys, Babe,' Fly had said, 'while I see to the sheep. I shan't be long.'

'What's sheep?' the piglet said when she had gone.

The puppies rolled about in the straw.

'Don't you know that, you silly Babe?' said one.

'Sheep are animals with thick woolly coats.'

'And thick woolly heads.'

'And men can't look after them without the help of the likes of us,' said the fourth.

'Why do they need you?' said Babe.

'Because we're sheep-dogs!' they all cried together, and ran off up the yard.

Babe thought about this matter of sheep and sheep-dogs a good deal during the first couple of weeks of his life on the Hoggets' farm. In that time Fly's puppies, now old enough to leave home, had been advertised for sale, and Fly was anxious to teach them all she could before they went out into the world. Daily she made them practise on the ducks, while Babe sat beside her and watched with interest. And daily their skills

improved and the ducks lost weight and patience.

Then there came, one after another, four farmers, four tall long-legged men who smelt of sheep. And each picked his puppy and paid his money, while Fly sat and watched her children leave to start their working life.

As always, she felt a pang to see each go, but this time, after the last had left, she was not alone.

'It's nice, dear,' she said to Babe. 'I've still got you.'

But not for all that long, she thought. Poor little chap, in six months or so he'll be fit to kill. At least he doesn't know it. She looked fondly at him, this foster-child that now called her 'Mum'. He had picked it up, naturally enough, from the puppies, but it pleased her to hear it, now more than ever.

'Mum,' said Babe.

'Yes, dear?'

'They've gone off to work sheep, haven't they?'

'Yes, dear.'

'Because they're sheep-dogs. Like you. You're useful to the boss, aren't you, because you're a sheep-dog?'

'Yes, dear.'

'Well, Mum?'

'Yes, dear?'

'Why can't I learn to be a sheep-pig?'

Four
'You'm a Polite Young Chap'

After the last of the puppies had left, the ducks heaved a general sigh of relief. They looked forward to a peaceful day and paid no attention when, the following morning, Fly and Babe came down to the pond and sat and watched them as they squattered and splattered in its soupy green depths. They knew that the old dog would not bother them, and they took no notice of the strange creature at her side.

'They'll come out and walk up the yard in a

minute,' said Fly. 'Then you can have a go at fetching them back, if you like.'

'Oh yes please!' said Babe excitedly.

The collie bitch looked fondly at her foster-child. Sheep-pig indeed, she thought, the idea of it! The mere sight of him would probably send the flock into the next county. Anyway he'd never get near them on those little short legs. Let him play with the ducks for a day or two and he'd forget all about it.

When the ducks did come up out of the water and marched noisily past the piglet, she half expected him to chase after them, as the puppies usually did at first; but he sat very still, his ears cocked, watching her.

'All right,' said Fly. 'Let's see how you get on. Now then, first thing is, you've got to get behind them, just like I have to with the sheep. If the boss wants me to go round the right side of them (that's the side by the stables there), he says "Away to me". If he wants me to go round the left (that's the side by the Dutch barn), he says

"Come by". OK?'

'Yes, Mum.'

'Right then. Away to me, Babe!' said Fly sharply.

At first, not surprisingly, Babe's efforts met with little success. There were no problems with getting round the ducks – even with his curious little see-sawing canter he was much faster than they – but the business of bringing the whole flock back to Fly was not, he found, at all easy.

Either he pressed them too hard and they broke up and fluttered all over the place, or he was too gentle and held back, and they waddled away in twos and threes.

'Come and have a rest, dear,' called Fly after a while. 'Leave the silly things alone, they're not worth upsetting yourself about.'

'I'm not upset, Mum,' said Babe. 'Just puzzled. I mean, I told them what I wanted them to do but they didn't take any notice of me. Why not?'

Because you weren't born to it, thought Fly. You haven't got the instinct to dominate them, to make them do what you want.

'It's early days yet, Babe dear,' she said.

'Do you suppose,' said Babe, 'that if I asked them politely . . .'

'Asked them politely! What an idea! Just imagine me doing that with the sheep – "please will you go through that gateway", "would you kindly walk into that pen?" Oh no, dear, you'd never get anywhere that way. You've got to tell 'em what to do, doesn't matter whether it's ducks or sheep. They're stupid and dogs are intelligent, that's what you have to remember.'

'But I'm a pig.'

'Pigs are intelligent too,' said Fly firmly. Ask them politely, she thought, whatever next!

What happened next, later that morning in fact, was that Babe met his first sheep.

Farmer Hogget and Fly had been out round the flock, and when they returned Fly was driving before her an old lame ewe, which they penned in the loose-box where the piglet had originally been shut. Then they went away up the hill again.

Babe made his way into the stables, curious to meet this, the first of the animals that he planned one day to work with, but he could not see into the box. He snuffled under the bottom of the door, and from inside there came a cough and the sharp stamp of a foot, and then the sound of a hoarse complaining voice. 'Wolves! Wolves!' it said. 'They do never leave a body alone. Nag, nag, nag all day long, go here, go there, do this, do that. What d'you want now? Can't you give us a bit of peace, wolf?'

'I'm not a wolf,' said Babe under the door.

'Oh, I knows all that,' said the sheep sourly. 'Calls yourself a sheep-dog, I knows that, but you don't fool none of us. You're a wolf like the rest of 'em, given half a chance. You looks at us, and you sees lamb-chops. Go away, wolf.'

'But I'm not a sheep-dog either,' said Babe, and he scrambled up the stack of straw bales and looked over the bars.

'You see?' he said.

'Well I'll be dipped,' said the old sheep, peering up at him, 'no more you ain't. What are you?'

'Pig,' said Babe. 'Large White. What are you?'

'Ewe,' said the sheep.

'No, not me, you – what are you?'

'I'm a ewe.'

Mum was right, thought Babe, they certainly are stupid. But if I'm going to learn how to be a sheep-pig I must try to understand them, and this might be a good chance. Perhaps I could make a friend of this one.

'My name's Babe,' he said in a jolly voice. 'What's yours?'

'Maaaaa,' said the sheep.

'That's a nice name,' said Babe. 'What's the matter with you, Ma?'

'Foot-rot,' said the sheep, holding up a foreleg. 'And I've got a nasty cough.' She coughed. 'And I'm not as young as I was.'

'You don't look very old to me,' said Babe politely.

A look of pleasure came over the sheep's mournful face, and she lay down in the straw.

'Very civil of you to say so,' she said. 'First kind word I've had since I were a little lamb,' and she belched loudly and began to chew a mouthful of cud.

Though he did not quite know why, Babe said nothing to Fly of his conversation with Ma. Farmer Hogget had treated the sheep's foot and tipped a drench down its protesting throat, and now, as darkness fell, dog and pig lay side by side, their rest only occasionally disturbed by a rustling from the next-door box. Having at last set eyes on a sheep, Babe's dreams were immediately filled with the creatures, all lame, all coughing, all, like the ducks, scattering wildly before his attempts to round them up.

'Go here, go there, do this, do that!' he squeaked furiously at them, but they took not a bit of notice, until at last the dream turned to nightmare, and they all came hopping and hacking and maa-ing after him with hatred gleaming in their mad yellow eyes.

'Mum! Mum!' shouted Babe in terror.

'Maaaaa!' said a voice next door.

'It's all right, dear,' said Fly, 'it's all right. Was it a nasty dream?'

'Yes, yes.'

'What were you dreaming about?'

'Sheep, Mum.'

'I expect it was because of that stupid old thing in there,' said Fly. 'Shut up!' she barked. 'Noisy old fool!' And to Babe she said, 'Now cuddle up, dear, and go to sleep. There's nothing to be frightened of.'

She licked his snout until it began to give out a series of regular snores. Sheep-pig indeed, she thought, why the silly boy's frightened of the things, and she put her nose on her paws and went to sleep.

*

Babe slept soundly the rest of the night, and woke more determined than ever to learn all that he could from their new neighbour. As soon as Fly had gone out on her rounds, he climbed the straw stack.

'Good morning, Ma,' he said. 'I do hope you're feeling better today?'

The old ewe looked up. Her eyes, Babe was glad to see, looked neither mad nor hateful.

'I must say,' she said, 'you'm a polite young chap. Not like that wolf, shouting at me in the middle of the night. Never get no respect from they, treat you like dirt they do, bite you soon as look at you.'

'Do they really?'

'Oh ar. Nip your hocks if you'm a bit slow. And worse, some of them.'

'Worse?'

'Oh ar. Ain't you never heard of worrying?'

'I don't worry much.'

'No no, young un. I'm talking about sheep-worrying. You get some wolves as'll chase sheep and kill 'em.'

'Oh!' said Babe, horrified. 'I'm sure Fly would never do that.'

'Who's Fly?'

'She's my m . . . she's our dog here, the one that brought you in yesterday.'

'Is that what she's called? No, she bain't a worrier, just rude. All wolves is rude to us sheep, see, always have been. Bark and run and nip and call us stupid. We bain't all that stupid, we do just get confused. If only they'd just show a bit of common politeness, just treat us a bit decent. Now if you was to come out into the field, a nice well-mannered young chap like you, and ask me to go somewhere or do something, politely, like you would, why, I'd be only too delighted.'

Five
'Keep Yelling, Young Un'

Mrs Hogget shook her head at least a dozen times.

'For the life of me I can't see why you do let that pig run all over the place like you do, round and round the yard he do go, chasing my ducks about, shoving his nose into everything, shouldn't wonder but what he'll be out with you and Fly moving the sheep about afore long, why dussen't shut him up, he's running all his flesh off, he won't never be fit for Christmas, Easter more like, what d'you call him?'

'Just Pig,' said Farmer Hogget.

A month had gone by since the Village Fair, a month in which a lot of interesting things had happened to Babe. The fact that perhaps most concerned his future, though he did not know it, was that Farmer Hogget had become fond of him. He liked to see the piglet pottering happily about the yard with Fly, keeping out of mischief, as far as he could tell, if you didn't count moving the ducks around. He did this now with a good deal of skill, the farmer noticed, even to the extent of being able, once, to separate the white ducks from the brown, though that must just have been a fluke. The more he thought of it, the less Farmer Hogget liked the idea of butchering Pig.

The other developments were in Babe's education. Despite herself, Fly found that she took pleasure and pride in teaching him the ways of the sheep-dog, though she knew that of course he would never be fast enough to work sheep.

Anyway the boss would never let him try.

As for Ma, she was back with the flock, her foot healed, her cough better. But all the time that she had been shut in the box, Babe had spent every moment that Fly was out of the stables chatting to the old ewe. Already he understood, in a way that Fly never could, the sheep's point of view. He longed to meet the flock, to be introduced. He thought it would be extremely interesting.

'D'you think I could, Ma?' he had said.

'Could what, young un?'

'Well, come and visit you, when you go back to your friends?'

'Oh ar. You could do, easy enough. You only got to go through the bottom gate and up the hill to the big field by the lane. Don't know what the farmer'd say though. Or that wolf.'

Once Fly had slipped quietly in and found him perched on the straw stack.

'Babe!' she had said sharply. 'You're not talking to that stupid thing, are you?'

'Well, yes, Mum, I was.'

'Save your breath, dear. It won't understand a word you say.'

'Bah!' said Ma.

For a moment Babe was tempted to tell his foster-mother what he had in mind, but something told him to keep quiet. Instead he made a plan. He would wait for two things to happen. First, for Ma to rejoin the flock. And after that for market day, when both the boss and his mum would be out of the way. Then he would go up the hill.

Towards the end of the very next week the two things had happened. Ma had been turned out, and a couple of days after that Babe watched as Fly jumped into the back of the Land Rover, and it drove out of the yard and away.

Babe's were not the only eyes that watched its departure. At the top of the hill a cattle-lorry stood half-hidden under a clump of trees at the side of the lane. As soon as the Land Rover had disappeared from sight along the road to the market town, a man jumped hurriedly out and opened the gate into the field. Another backed the lorry into the gateway.

Babe meanwhile was trotting excitedly up the hill to pay his visit to the flock. He came to the gate at the bottom of the field and squeezed under it. The field was steep and curved, and at first he could not see a single sheep. But then he heard a distant drumming of hooves and suddenly the whole flock came galloping over the brow of the hill and down towards him. Around them ran two strange collies, lean silent dogs that seemed to flow effortlessly over the grass. From high above came the sound of a thin whistle, and in easy partnership the dogs swept round the sheep, and began to drive them back up the slope.

Despite himself, Babe was caught up in the press of jostling bleating animals and carried along with them. Around him rose a chorus of panting protesting voices, some shrill, some hoarse, some deep and guttural, but all saying the same thing.

'Wolf! Wolf!' cried the flock in dazed confusion.

Small by comparison and short in the leg, Babe soon fell behind the main body, and as they reached the top of the hill he found himself right at the back in company with an old sheep who cried 'Wolf!' more loudly than any.

'Ma!' he cried breathlessly. 'It's you!'

Behind them one dog lay down at a whistle, and in front the flock checked as the other dog steadied them. In the corner of the field the tailboard and wings of the cattle-lorry filled the gateway, and the two men waited, sticks and arms outspread.

'Oh hullo, young un,' puffed the old sheep. 'Fine day you chose to come, I'll say.'

'What is it? What's happening? Who are these men?' asked Babe.

'Rustlers,' said Ma. 'They'm sheep-rustlers.'

'What d'you mean?'

'Thieves, young un, that's what I do mean. Sheep-stealers. We'll all be in thik lorry afore you can blink your eye.'

'What can we do?'

'Do? Ain't nothing we can do, unless we can slip past theseyer wolf.'

She made as if to escape, but the dog behind darted in, and she turned back.

Again, one of the men whistled, and the dog pressed. Gradually, held against the headland of the field by the second dog and the men, the flock began to move forward. Already the leaders were nearing the tailboard of the lorry.

'We'm beat,' said Ma mournfully. 'You run for it, young un.' I will, thought Babe, but not the way you mean. Little as he was, he felt suddenly not fear but anger, furious anger that the boss's sheep were being stolen. My mum's not here to protect them so I must, he said to himself bravely, and he ran quickly round the hedge side of the flock, and jumping on to the bottom of the tailboard, turned to face them.

'Please!' he cried. 'I beg you! Please don't come any further. If you would be so kind, dear sensible sheep!'

His unexpected appearance had a number of immediate effects. The shock of being so politely addressed stopped the flock in its tracks, and the cries of 'Wolf!' changed to murmurs of 'In't he lovely!' and 'Proper little gennulman!' Ma had told them something of her new friend, and now to see him in the flesh and to hear his well-chosen words released them from the dominance of the dogs. They began to fidget and look about for an escape route. This was opened for them when the men (cursing quietly, for above all things they were anxious to avoid too much noise) sent the flanking dog to drive the pig away, and some of the sheep began to slip past them.

Next moment all was chaos. Angrily the dog ran at Babe, who scuttled away squealing at the top of his voice in a mixture of fright and fury. The men closed on him, sticks raised. Desperately he shot between the legs of one, who fell with a crash, while the other, striking out madly, hit the rearguard dog as it came to help, and sent it yowling. In half a minute the carefully planned raid was ruined, as the sheep scattered everywhere.

'Keep yelling, young un!' bawled Ma, as she ran beside Babe. 'They won't never stop here with that row going on!'

And suddenly all sorts of things began to happen as those deafening squeals rang out over the quiet countryside. Birds flew startled from the trees, cows in nearby fields began to gallop about, dogs in distant farms to bark, passing motorists to stop and stare. In the farmhouse below, Mrs Hogget heard the noise as she had on the day of the Fair, but now it was infinitely louder, the most piercing, nerve-tingling, ear-shattering burglar alarm. She dialled 999 but then talked for so long that, by the time a patrol car drove up the lane, the rustlers had long gone. Snarling at each other and their dogs, they had driven hurriedly away with not one single sheep to show for their pains.

'You won't never believe it!' cried Mrs Hogget when her husband returned from market. 'But we've had rustlers, just after you'd gone it were, come with a girt cattle-lorry they did, the police said, they seen the tyremarks in the gateway, and a chap in a car seen the lorry go by in a hurry, and there's been a lot of it about, and he give the alarm, he did, kept screaming and shrieking enough to bust your eardrums, we should have lost every sheep on the place if 'tweren't for him, 'tis him we've got to thank.'

'Who?' said Farmer Hogget.

'Him!' said his wife, pointing at Babe who was telling Fly all about it. 'Don't ask me how he got there or why he done it, all I knows is he saved our bacon and now I'm going to save his, he's stopping with us just like another dog, don't care if he gets so big as a house, because if you think I'm going to stand by and see him butchered after what he done for us today, you've got another think coming, what d'you say to that?'

A slow smile spread over Farmer Hogget's long face.

Six
'Good Pig'

The very next morning Farmer Hogget decided that he would see if the pig would like to come, when he went round the sheep with Fly. I'm daft, he thought, grinning to himself. He did not tell his wife.

Seeing him walk down the yard, crook in hand, and hearing him call Fly, Babe was about to settle down for an after-breakfast nap when to his surprise he heard the farmer's voice again.

'Come, Pig,' said Farmer Hogget and to his surprise the pig came.

'I expect it's because of what you did yesterday,' said Fly proudly, as they walked to heel together up the hill. 'The boss must be very pleased with you, dear. You can watch me working.'

When they reached the lower gate, Farmer Hogget opened it and left it open.

'He's going to bring them down into the home paddock, away from the lane,' said Fly quickly. 'You be quiet and keep out of the way,' and she went to sit waiting by the farmer's right side.

'Come by!' he said, and Fly ran left up the slope as the sheep began to bunch above her. Once behind them, she addressed them in her usual way, that is to say sharply.

'Move, fools!' she snapped. 'Down the hill. If you know which way "down" is,' but to her surprise they did not obey. Instead they turned to face her, and some even stamped, and shook their heads at her, while a great chorus of bleating began.

To Fly sheep-talk was just so much rubbish, to which she had never paid any attention, but Babe, listening below, could hear clearly what was being said, and although the principal cry was the usual one, there were other voices saying other things. The contrast between the politeness with which they had been treated by yesterday's rescuer and the everlasting rudeness to which they were subjected by this or any wolf brought mutinous thoughts into woolly heads, and words of defiance rang out.

'You got no manners! . . . Why can't you ask nicely? . . . Treat us like muck, you do!' they cried, and one hoarse voice which the pig recognized called loudly, 'We don't want you, wolf. We want Babe!' whereupon they all took it up.

'We want Babe!' they bleated. 'Babe! Babe! Ba-a-a-a-a-be!'

Those behind pushed at those in front, so that

they actually edged a pace or two nearer the dog.

For a moment it seemed to Babe that Fly was not going to be able to move them, that she would lose this particular battle of wills; but he had not reckoned with her years of experience. Suddenly, quick as a flash, she drove in on them with a growl and with a twisting leap sprang for the nose of the foremost animal; Babe heard the clack of her teeth as the ewe fell over backwards in fright, a fright which immediately ran through all. Defiant no longer, the flock poured down the hill, Fly snapping furiously at their heels, and surged wildly through the gateway.

'No manners! No manners! No ma-a-a-a-anners!' they cried, but an air of panic ran through them as they realized how rebellious they had been. How the wolf would punish them! They ran helter-skelter into the middle of the paddock, and wheeled as one to look back, ears pricked, eyes wide with fear. They puffed and blew, and Ma's hacking cough rang out. But to their surprise they saw that the wolf had dropped by the gateway, and that after a moment the pig came trotting out to one side of them.

Though Farmer Hogget could not know what had caused the near-revolt of the flock, he saw clearly that for some reason they had given Fly a hard time, and that she was angry. It was not like her to gallop sheep in that pell-mell fashion.

'Steady!' he said curtly as she harried the rearguard, and then 'Down!' and 'Stay!' and shut the gate. Shepherding suited Farmer Hogget – there was no waste of words in it.

In the corner of the home paddock nearest to

the farm buildings was a smallish fenced yard divided into a number of pens and runways. Here the sheep would be brought at shearing-time or to pick out fat lambs for market or to be treated for various troubles. Farmer Hogget had heard the old ewe cough; he thought he would catch her up and give her another drench. He turned to give an order to Fly lying flat and still behind him, and there, lying flat and still beside her, was the pig.

'Stay, Fly!' said Hogget. And, just for fun, 'Come, Pig!'

Immediately Babe ran forward and sat at the farmer's right, his front trotters placed neatly together, his big ears cocked for the next command.

Strange thoughts began to stir in Farmer Hogget's mind, and unconsciously he crossed his fingers.

He took a deep breath, and, holding it . . . 'Away to me, Pig!' he said softly.

Without a moment's hesitation Babe began the long outrun to the right.

Quite what Farmer Hogget had expected to happen, he could never afterwards clearly remember. What he had not expected was that the pig would run round to the rear of the flock, and turn to face it and him, and lie down instantly without a word of further command spoken, just as a well-trained dog would have done. Admittedly, with his jerky little rocking-horse canter he took twice as long to get there as Fly would have, but still, there he was, in the right place, ready and waiting. Admittedly, the sheep had turned to face the pig and were making a great deal of noise, but then Farmer Hogget did not know, and Fly would not listen to, what they were saying. He called the dog to heel, and began to walk with his long loping stride to the collecting-pen in the corner. Out in the middle of the paddock there was a positive babble of talk.

'Good morning!' said Babe. 'I do hope I find you all well, and not too distressed by yesterday's experience?' and immediately it seemed that every sheep had something to say to him.

'Bless his heart!' they cried, and, 'Dear little soul!' and, 'Hullo, Babe!' and, 'Nice to see you again!' and then there was a rasping cough and the sound of Ma's hoarse tones.

'What's up then, young un?' she croaked.

'What be you doing here instead of that wolf?'

Although Babe wanted, literally, to keep on the right side of the sheep, his loyalty to his foster-mother made him say in a rather hurt voice, 'She's not a wolf. She's a sheep-dog.'

'Oh all right then,' said Ma, 'sheep-dog, if you must have it. What dost want, then?'

Babe looked at the army of long sad faces.

'I want to be a sheep-pig,' he said.

'Ha ha!' bleated a big lamb standing next to Ma. 'Ha ha ha-a-a-a-a!'

'Bide quiet!' said Ma sharply, swinging her head to give the lamb a thumping butt in the side. 'That ain't nothing to laugh at.'

Raising her voice, she addressed the flock.

'Listen to me, all you ewes,' she said, 'and lambs too. This young chap was kind to me, like I told you, when I were poorly. And I told him, if he was to ask me to go somewhere or do something, politely, like he would, why, I'd be only too delighted. We ain't stupid, I told him, all we do want is to be treated right, and we'm as bright as the next beast, we are.'

'We are!' chorused the flock. 'We are! We are! We a-a-a-a-a-are!'

'Right then,' said Ma. 'What shall us do, Babe?'

Babe looked across towards Farmer Hogget, who had opened the gate of the collecting-pen and now stood leaning on his crook, Fly at his feet. The pen was in the left bottom corner of the paddock, and so Babe expected, and at that moment got, the command 'Come by, Pig!' to send him left and so behind the sheep and thus turn them down towards the corner.

He cleared his throat. 'If I might ask a great favour of you,' he said hurriedly, 'could you all please be kind enough to walk down to that gate where the farmer is standing, and to go through it? Take your time, please, there's absolutely no rush.'

A look of pure contentment passed over the faces of the flock, and with one accord they turned and walked across the paddock, Babe a few paces in their rear. Sedately they walked, and steadily, over to the corner, through the gate, into the pen, and then stood quietly waiting. No one broke ranks or tried to slip away, no one pushed or shoved, there was no noise or fuss. From the oldest to the youngest, they went in like lambs.

Then at last a gentle murmur broke out as everyone in different ways quietly expressed their pleasure.

'Babe!' said Fly to the pig. 'That was quite beautifully done, dear!'

'Thank you so much!' said Babe to the sheep. 'You did that so nicely!'

'Ta!' said the sheep. 'Ta! Ta! Ta-a-a-a-a-a! 'Tis a pleasure to work for such a

little gennulman!' And Ma added, 'You'll make a wunnerful sheep-pig, young un, or my name's not Ma-a-a-a-a.'

As for Farmer Hogget, he heard none of this, so wrapped up was he in his own thoughts. He's as good as a dog, he told himself excitedly, he's better than a dog, than any dog! I wonder . . . !

'Good Pig,' he said.

Then he uncrossed his fingers and closed the gate.

Seven
'What's Trials?'

Every day after that, of course, Babe went the rounds with Farmer Hogget and Fly. At first the farmer worried about using the pig to herd the sheep, not because it was a strange and unusual thing to do which people might laugh at – he did not care about that – but because he was afraid it might upset Fly and put her nose out of joint. However it did not seem to do so.

He could have spared himself the worry if he had been able to listen to their conversation.

'That *was* fun!' said Babe to Fly that evening. 'I wonder if the boss will let me do some more work?'

'I'm sure he will, dear. You did it so well. It was almost as though the sheep knew exactly what it was you wanted them to do.'

'But that's just it! I asked them . . .'

'No use asking sheep anything, dear,' interrupted Fly. 'You have to *make* them do what you want, I've told you before.'

'Yes, Mum. But . . . will you mind, if the boss uses me instead of you, sometimes?'

'Mind?' said Fly. 'You bet your trotters I won't! All my life I've had to run round after those idiots, up hill, down dale, day in, day out. And as for "sometimes", as far as I'm concerned you can work them every day. I'm not as young as I was. I'll be only too happy to lie comfortably in the grass and watch you, my Babe.'

And before long that was exactly what she was doing. Once Farmer Hogget could see by her wagging tail and smiling eyes that she was perfectly happy about it, he began to use Babe to do some of her work. At first he only gave the pig simple tasks, but as the days and weeks went by, Hogget began to make more and more use of his new helper. The speed with which Babe learned amazed him, and before long he was relying on him for all the work with the flock, while Fly lay and proudly watched. Now, there was nothing, it seemed, that the pig could not do, and do faultlessly, at that.

He obeyed all the usual commands immediately and correctly. He could fetch sheep or take them away, move them to left or right, persuade them round obstacles or through gaps, cut the flock in half, or take out one individual.

To drench Ma, for instance, there was no need for Hogget to bring all the sheep down to the collecting-pen, or to corner them all and catch her by a hindleg with his crook. He could simply point her out to the pig, and Babe would gently work her out of the bunch and bring her right to the farmer's feet, where she stood quietly waiting. It seemed like a miracle to Hogget, but of course it was simple.

'Ma!'

'Yes, young un?'

'The boss wants to give you some more medicine.'

'Oh not again! 'Tis horrible stuff, that.'

'But it'll make your cough better.'

'Oh ar?'

'Come along, Ma. Please.'

'Oh all right then, young un. Anything to oblige you.'

And there were other far more miraculous

things that Babe could easily have done if the farmer had only known. For example when it was time for the ewes to be separated from their lambs, now almost as big and strong as their mothers, Farmer Hogget behaved like any other shepherd, and brought the whole flock down to the pens, and took a lot of time and trouble to part them. If only he had been able to explain things to Babe, how easy it could have been.

'Dear ladies, will you please stay on the hill, if you'd be so kind?'

'Youngsters, down you go to the collecting-pen if you please, there's good boys and girls,' and it could have been done in the shake of a lamb's tail.

However, Babe's increasing skill at working sheep determined Farmer Hogget to take the next step in a plan which had begun to form in his mind on the day when the piglet had first penned the sheep. That step was nothing less than to take Pig with him to the local sheep-dog trials in a couple of weeks' time. Only just to watch, of course, just so that he could have a look at well-trained dogs working a small number of sheep, and see what they and their handlers were required to do. I'm daft, he thought, grinning to himself. He did not tell his wife.

Before the day came, he put a collar and lead on the pig. He could not risk him running away, in a strange place. He kept him on the lead all one morning, letting Fly do the work as of old. He need not have bothered – Babe would have stayed tight at heel when told – but it was interesting to note the instant change in the atmosphere as the collie ran out.

'Wolf! Wolf!' cried the flock, every sheep immediately on edge.

'Move, fools!' snapped Fly, and she hustled them and bustled them with little regard for their feelings.

'Babe! We want Babe!' they bleated. 'Ba-a-a-a-a-a-be!'

To be sure, the work was done more quickly, but at the end of it the sheep were in fear and trembling and the dog out of patience and breath.

'Steady! Steady!' called the farmer a number of times, something he never had to say to Babe.

When the day came for the local trials, Farmer Hogget set off early in the Land Rover, Fly and Babe in the back. He told his wife where he was going, though not that he was taking the pig. Nor

did he say that he did not intend to be an ordinary spectator, but instead more of a spy, to see without being seen. He wanted Pig to observe everything that went on without being spotted. Now that he had settled on the final daring part of his plan, Hogget realized that secrecy was all-important. No one must know that he owned a . . . what would you call him, he thought . . . a sheep-pig, I suppose!

The trials took place ten miles or so away, in a curved basin-shaped valley in the hills. At the lower end of the basin was a road. Close to this was the starting point, where the dogs would begin their outrun, and also the enclosure where they would finally pen their sheep. Down there all the spectators would gather. Farmer Hogget, arriving some time before them, parked the Land Rover in a lane, and set off up the valley by a roundabout way, keeping in the shelter of the bordering woods, Fly padding behind him and Babe on the lead trotting to keep up with his long strides.

'Where are we going, Mum?' said Babe excitedly. 'What are we going to do?'

'I don't think we're going to do anything, dear,' said Fly. 'I think the boss wants you to see something.'

'What?'

They had reached the head of the valley now, and the farmer found a suitable place to stop, under cover, but with a good view of the course.

'Down, Fly, down, Pig, and stay,' he said and exhausted by this long speech, stretched his long frame on the ground and settled down to wait.

'Wants me to see what?' said Babe.

'The trials.'

'What's trials?'

'Well,' said Fly, 'it's a sort of competition, for sheep-dogs and their bosses. Each dog has to fetch five sheep, and move them through a number of gaps and gateways – you can see which ones, they've got flags on either side – down to that circle that's marked out in the field right at the bottom, and there the dog has to shed some sheep.'

'What's "shed" mean?'

'Separate them out from the rest; the ones to be shed will have collars on.'

'And then what?'

'Then the dog has to gather them all again, and pen them.'

'Is that all?'

'It's not easy, dear. Not like moving that bunch of woolly fools of ours up and down a field. It all has to be done quickly, without any mistakes. You lose points if you make mistakes.'

'Have you ever been in a trial, Mum?'

'Yes. Here. When I was younger.'

'Did you make any mistakes?'

'Of course,' said Fly. 'Everyone does. It's very difficult, working a small number of strange sheep, in strange country. You'll see.'

By the end of the day Babe had seen a great deal. The course was not an easy one, and the sheep were very different from those at home. They were fast and wild, and, good though the dogs were, there were many mistakes made, at the gates, in the shedding-ring, at the final penning.

Babe watched every run intently, and Hogget watched Babe, and Fly watched them both.

What's the boss up to, she thought, as they drove home. He's surely never thinking that one day Babe might . . . no, he couldn't be that daft! Sheep-pig indeed! All right for the little chap to run round our place for a bit of fun, but to think of him competing in trials, even a little local one like today's, well, really! She remembered something he had said in his early duck-herding days.

'I suppose you'd say,' she remarked, 'that those dogs just weren't polite enough?'

'That's right,' said Babe.

Eight
'Oh Ma!'

Fly's suspicions about what the farmer was up to grew rapidly over the next weeks. It soon became obvious to her that he was constructing, on his own land, a practice course. From the top of the field where the rustlers had come, the circuit which he laid out ran all round the farm, studded with hazards to be negotiated. Some were existing gateways or gaps. Some he made, with hurdles, or lines of posts between which the sheep had to be driven. Some were extremely difficult. One, for example, a plank bridge over a stream, was so narrow that it could only be crossed in single file, and the most honeyed words were needed from Babe to persuade the animals to cross.

Then, in the home paddock, Hogget made a rough shedding-ring with a circle of large stones, and beyond it, a final pen, a small hurdle enclosure no bigger than a tiny room, with a gate to close its mouth when he pulled on a rope.

Every day the farmer would send Fly to cut out five sheep from the flock, and take them to the top of the hill, and hold them there. Then, starting Babe from the gate at the lower end of the farmyard, Hogget would send him away to run them through the course.

'Away to me, Pig!' he would say, or 'Come by, Pig!' and off Babe would scamper as fast as his trotters could carry him, as the farmer pulled out his big old pocket watch and noted the time. There was only one problem. His trotters wouldn't carry him all that fast.

Here at home, Fly realized, his lack of speed didn't matter much. Whichever five sheep were selected were only too anxious to oblige Babe, and would hurry eagerly to do whatever he wanted. But with strange sheep it will be different, thought Fly. If the boss really does intend to run him in a trial. Which it looks as though he does! She watched his tubby pinky-white shape as he crested the hill.

That evening at suppertime she watched again as he tucked into his food. Up till now it had never worried her how much he ate. He's a growing boy, she had thought fondly. Now she thought, he's a greedy boy too.

'Babe,' she said, as with a grunt of content he licked the last morsels off the end of his snout. His little tin trough was as shiningly clean as though Mrs Hogget had washed it in her sink, and his tummy was as tight as a drum.

'Yes, Mum?'

'You like being a . . . sheep-pig, don't you?'

'Oh yes, Mum!'

'And you'd like to be really good at it, wouldn't you? The greatest? Better than any other sheep-pig?'

'D'you think there are any others?'

'Well, no. Better than any sheep-dog, then?'

'Oh yes, I'd love to be! But I don't really think that's possible. You see, although sheep do seem to go very well for me, and do what I ask . . . I mean, do what I tell them, I'm nothing like as fast as a dog and never could be.'

'No. But you could be a jolly sight faster than you are.'

'How?'

'Well, there are two things you'd have to do, dear,' said Fly. 'First, you'd have to go into proper training. One little run around a day's not enough. You'd have to practise hard – jogging, cross-country running, sprinting, distance work. I'd help you of course.'

It all sounded fun to Babe.

'Great!' he said. 'But you said "two things". What's the second?'

'Eat less,' said Fly. 'You'd have to go on a diet.'

Any ordinary pig would have rebelled at this point. Pigs enjoy eating, and they also enjoy lying around most of the day thinking about eating again. But Babe was no ordinary pig, and he set out enthusiastically to do what Fly suggested.

Under her
watchful eye he
ate wisely but
not too well, and
every afternoon
he trained, to a programme which she had
worked out, trotting right round the boundaries
of the farm perhaps, or running up to the top of
the hill and back again, or racing up and down
the home paddock. Hogget thought that Pig was
just playing, but he couldn't help noticing how
he had grown; not fatter, as a sty-kept pig would
have done, but stronger and wirier. There was
nothing of the piglet about him any more; he
looked lean and racy and hard-muscled, and
he was now almost as
big as the sheep he
herded. And the
day came when that
strength and hardness
were to stand him
in good stead.

*

One beautiful morning, when the sky was clear and cloudless, and the air so crisp and fresh that you could almost taste it, Babe woke feeling on top of the world. Like a trained athlete, he felt so charged with energy that he simply couldn't keep still. He bounced about the stable floor on all four feet, shaking his head about and uttering a series of short sharp squeaks.

'You're full of it this morning,' said Fly with a yawn. 'You'd better run to the top of the hill and back to work it off.'

'OK, Mum!' said Babe, and off he shot while Fly settled comfortably back in the straw.

Dashing across the home paddock, Babe bounded up the hill and looked about for the sheep. Though he knew he would see them later on, he felt so pleased with life that he thought he would like to share that feeling with Ma and all the others, before he ran home again; just to say 'Hullo! Good morning, everybody! Isn't it a lovely day!' They were, he knew, in the most distant of all the fields on the farm, right away up at the top of the lane.

He looked across, expecting that they would be grazing quietly or lying comfortably and cudding in the morning sun, only to see them galloping madly in every direction. On the breeze came cries of 'Wolf!' but not in the usual bored, almost automatic, tones of complaint that they used when Fly worked them. These were yells of real terror, desperate calls for help. As he watched, two other animals came in sight, one large, one small, and he heard the sound of barking and yapping as they dashed about after the fleeing sheep. 'You get some wolves as'll chase sheep and kill 'em' – Ma's exact words came back to Babe, and without a second thought he set off as fast as he could go in the direction of the noise.

What a sight greeted him when he arrived in the far field! The flock, usually so tightly bunched, was scattered everywhere, eyes bulging, mouths open, heads hanging in their evident distress, and it was clear that the dogs had been at their worrying for some time. A few sheep had tried in their terror to jump the wire fencing and had become caught up in it, some had fallen into the ditches and got stuck. Some were limping as they ran about, and on the grass were lumps of wool torn from others.

Most dreadful of all, in the middle of the field, the worriers had brought down a ewe, which lay on its side feebly kicking at them as they growled and tugged at it.

On the day when the rustlers had come, Babe had felt a mixture of fear and anger. Now he knew nothing but a blind rage, and he charged flat out at the two dogs, grunting and snorting with fury. Nearest to him was the smaller dog, a kind of mongrel terrier, which was snapping at one of the ewe's hindlegs, deaf to everything in the excitement of the worry.

Before it could move, Babe took it across the back and flung it to one side, and the force of his rush carried him on into the bigger dog and knocked it flying.

This one, a large black crossbred, part collie, part retriever, was made of sterner stuff than the terrier, which was already running dazedly away; and it picked itself up and came snarling back at the pig. Perhaps, in the confusion of the moment, it thought that this was just another sheep that had somehow found courage to attack it; but if so, it soon knew better, for as it came on, Babe chopped at it with his terrible pig's bite, the bite that grips and tears, and now it was not sheep's blood that was spilled.

Howling in pain, the black dog turned and ran, his tail between his legs. He ran, in fact, for his life, an open-mouthed bristling pig hard on his heels.

The field was clear, and Babe suddenly came back to his senses. He turned and hurried to the fallen ewe, round whom, now that the dogs had gone, the horrified flock was beginning to gather in a rough circle. She lay still now, as Babe stood panting by her side, a draggled side where the worriers had pulled at it, and suddenly he realized. It was Ma!

'Ma!' he cried. 'Ma! Are you all right?'
She did not seem too badly hurt. He could not see any gaping wounds, though blood was coming from one ear where the dogs had bitten it.

The old ewe opened an eye. Her voice, when she spoke, was as hoarse as ever, but now not much more than a whisper.

'Hullo, young un,' she said.

Babe dropped his head and gently licked the ear to try to stop the bleeding, and some blood stuck to his snout.

'Can you get up?' he asked.

For some time Ma did not answer, and he looked anxiously at her, but the eye that he could see was still open.

'I don't reckon,' she said.

'It's all right, Ma,' Babe said. 'The wolves have gone, far away.'

'Far, far, fa-a-a-a-ar!' chorused the flock.

'And Fly and the boss will soon be here to look after you.'

Ma made no answer or movement. Only her ribs jumped to the thump of her tired old heart.

'You'll be all right, honestly you will,' said Babe.

'Oh ar,' said Ma, and then the eye closed and the ribs jumped no more.

'Oh Ma!' said Babe, and 'Ma! Ma! Ma-a-a-a-a-a!' mourned the flock, as the Land Rover came up the lane.

Farmer Hogget had heard nothing of the worrying – the field was too far away, the wind in the wrong direction – but he had been anxious, and so by now had Fly, because Pig was nowhere to be found.

The moment they entered the field both man and dog could see that something was terribly wrong. Why else was the flock so obviously distressed, panting and gasping and dishevelled?

Why had they formed that ragged circle, and what was in the middle of it? Farmer Hogget strode forward, Fly before him parting the ring to make way, only to see a sight that struck horror into the hearts of both.

There before them lay a dead ewe, and bending over it was the pig, his snout almost touching the outstretched neck, a snout, they saw, that was stained with blood.

Nine
'Was It Babe?'

'Go home, Pig!' said Farmer Hogget in a voice that was so quiet and cold that Babe hardly recognized it. Bewildered, he trotted off obediently, while behind him the farmer picked up the dead ewe and carried it to the Land Rover. Then with Fly's help he began the task of rescuing those sheep that were caught or stuck, and of making sure that no others were badly hurt. This done, he left Fly to guard the flock, and drove home.

*

Back at the farm, Babe felt simply very very sad.
The sky was still cloudless, the air still crisp, but
this was a very different pig from the one that
had cantered carefree up the hill not half an hour
ago. In those thirty minutes he had seen naked
fear and cruelty and death, and now
to cap it all, the boss was angry
with him, had sent him home in
some sort of disgrace. What had
he done wrong? He had only
done his duty, as a good sheep-
pig should. He sat in the
doorway of the stables and
watched as the Land Rover
drove into the yard, poor
Ma's head lolling loosely
over the back. He saw the
boss get out and go into
the house, and then, a few
minutes later, come out again,
carrying something in the crook

of one arm, a long thing, a kind of black shiny tube, and walk towards him.

'Come, Pig,' said Farmer Hogget in that same cold voice, and strode past him into the stables, while at the same moment, inside the farmhouse, the telephone began to ring, and then stopped as Mrs Hogget picked it up.

Obediently Babe followed the farmer into the dark interior. It was not so dark however that he could not see clearly that the boss was pointing the black shiny tube at him, and he sat down again and waited, supposing that perhaps it was some machine for giving out food and that some quite unexpected surprise would come out of its two small round mouths, held now quite close to his face.

At that instant Mrs Hogget's voice sounded across the yard, calling her husband's name from the open kitchen window. He frowned, lowered the shiny tube, and poked his head around the stable door.

'Oh there you are!' called Mrs Hogget. 'What

dost think then, that was the police that was, they'm ringing every farmer in the district to warn 'em, there's sheep-worrying dogs about, they killed six sheep t'other side of the valley only last night, they bin seen they have, two of 'em 'tis, a big black un and a little brown un, they say to shoot 'em on sight if you do see 'em, you better get back up the hill and make sure ours is all right, d'you want me to fetch your gun?'

'No,' said Farmer Hogget. 'It's all right,' he said.

He waited till his wife had shut the window and disappeared, and then he walked out into the sunlight with Babe following.

'Sit, Pig,' he said, but now his voice was warm and kindly again.

He looked closely at the trusting face turned up to his, and saw, sticking to the side of Babe's mouth, some hairs, some black hairs, and a few brown ones too.

He shook his head in wonder, and that slow grin spread over his face.

'I reckon you gave them summat to worry about,' he said, and he broke the gun and took out the cartridges.

Meanwhile Fly, standing guard up in the far field, was terribly agitated. She knew of course that some dogs will attack sheep, sometimes even the very dogs trained to look after them, but surely not her sheep-pig? Surely Babe could not have done such a thing? Yet there he had been at the centre of that scene of chaos, bloodstained and standing over a dead ewe! What would the boss do to him, what perhaps had he already done? Yet she could not leave these fools to find out.

At least though, she suddenly realized, they could tell her what had happened, if the shock hadn't driven what little sense they had out of their stupid heads. Never before in her long life had Fly sunk to engaging a sheep in conversation.

They were there to be ordered about, like soldiers, and, like soldiers, never to answer back. She approached the nearest one, with distaste, and it promptly backed away from her.

'Stand still, fool!' she barked. 'And tell me who chased you. Who killed that old one?'

'Wolf,' said the sheep automatically.

Fly growled with annoyance. Was that the only word the halfwits knew? She put the question differently.

'Was it the pig that chased you? Was it Babe?' she said.

'Ba-a-a-a-abe!' bleated the sheep eagerly.

'What does that mean, bonehead?' barked Fly. 'Was it or wasn't it?'

'Wolf,' said the sheep.

Somehow Fly controlled her anger at the creature's stupidity. I *must* know what happened, she thought. Babe's always talking about being polite to these woolly idiots. I'll have to try it. I must know. She took a deep breath.

'Please . . .' she said. The sheep, which had

begun to graze, raised its head sharply and stared
at her with an expression of total amazement.

'Say that agai-ai-ai-ain,' it said, and a number
of others, overhearing, moved towards the
collie.

'Please,' said Fly, swallowing hard, 'could you
be kind enough to tell me.'

'Hark!' interrupted the first sheep. 'Hark! Ha-
a-a-a-ark!' whereupon
the whole flock ran
and gathered round.
They stood in silence, every
eye fixed wonderingly on
her, every mouth hanging

open. Nincompoops! thought Fly. Just when I wanted to ask one quietly the whole fat-headed lot come round. But I must know. I must know the truth about my Babe, however terrible it is.

'Please,' she said once more in a voice choked with the effort of being humble, 'could you be kind enough to tell me what happened this morning? Did Babe . . . ?' but she got no further, for at the mention of the pig's name the whole flock burst out into a great cry of 'Ba-a-a-abe!'

Listening, for the first time ever, to what the sheep were actually saying, Fly could hear individual voices competing to make themselves heard, in what was nothing less than a hymn of praise. 'Babe ca-a-a-aame!' 'He sa-a-a-aved us!' 'He drove the wolves awa-a-a-ay!' 'He made them pa-a-a-a-ay!' 'Hip hip hooray! Hip hip hooray! Hip hip hoora-a-a-ay!'

What a sense of relief flooded over her as she heard and understood the words of the sheep! It had been sheep-worriers, after all! And her boy had come to the rescue! He was not the villain, he was the hero!

Hogget and Babe heard the racket as they climbed the hill, and the farmer sent the pig ahead, fearing that perhaps the worriers had returned.

Under cover of the noise Babe arrived on the scene unnoticed by Fly, just in time to hear her reply.

'Oh thank you!' she cried to the flock. 'Thank you all so much for telling me! How kind of you!'

'Gosh, Mum,' said a voice behind her. 'What's come over you?'

Ten

'Get It Off By Heart'

Because Babe had now saved the flock not only from rustlers but also from the worriers, the Hoggets could not do too much for him.

Because he was a pig (though Farmer Hogget increasingly found himself thinking of Pig as Dog and fed him accordingly), they gave him unlimited supplies of what they supposed he could not have too much of – namely, food.

Because he was strong-minded and revelled in his newfound speed, he ate sparingly of it.

Because there was always a lot left over, Fly became fat and the chickens chubby and the ducks dumpy, and the very rats and mice rolled happily about the stables with stomachs full to bursting.

Mrs Hogget even took to calling Babe to the back door, to feed him some titbit or other that she thought he might particularly fancy; and from here it was but a short step to inviting him into the house, which one day she did.

When the farmer came in for his tea, he found not only Fly but also Pig lying happily asleep beside the Aga cooker. And afterwards, when he sat down in his armchair in the sitting-room and switched

on the television, Babe came to sit beside him, and they watched the six o'clock news together.

'He likes it,' said Hogget to his wife when she came into the room. Mrs Hogget nodded her head a great many times, and as usual had a few words to say on the subject.

'Dear little chap, though you can't call him little no longer, he've growed so much, why, he's big enough to you-know-what, not that we ever shall now, over my dead body though I hopes it ain't if you see what I do mean, just look at him, we should have brought him in the house long ago, no reason why not, is there now?'

'He might mess the carpet,' said Farmer Hogget.

'Never!' cried Mrs Hogget, shaking her head the entire time that she was speaking. 'He's no more likely to mess than he is to fly, he'll ask to go out when he wants to do his do's, just like a good clean dog would, got more brains than a dog he has, why 'twouldn't surprise me to hear he was rounding up them old sheep of yourn, 'twouldn't honestly, though I suppose you think I'm daft?'

Farmer Hogget grinned to himself. He did not tell his wife what she had never yet noticed, that all the work of the farm was now done by the sheep-pig. And he had no intention of telling her of the final part of his plan, which was nothing less than to enter Pig in that sternest of all tests, the Grand Challenge Sheep Dog Trials, open to all comers! Never in his working life had he owned an animal good enough to compete in these Trials. Now at last he had one, and he was not going to be stopped from realizing his ambition by the fact that it was a pig.

In a couple of weeks they would be competing against the best sheep-dogs in the country, would be appearing, in fact, on that very television screen they were now watching.

'No, you're not daft,' he said.

But you won't half get a surprise when you sit here and watch it, he thought. And so will a lot of other folks.

His plan was simple. He would appear at the Grand Challenge Trials with Fly, and at the last possible moment swap her for Pig. By then it would be too late for anyone to stop him. It didn't matter what happened afterwards – they could disqualify him, fine him, send him to prison, anything – as long as he could run Pig, just one glorious run, just to show them all!

And they couldn't say they hadn't been warned – the name was there on the entry form.

He had been worried, for he was a truthful man, that the heading might say 'Name of Dog', and then whatever he put would be a lie. But he'd been lucky. 'Name of Competitor' (the form said) . . .

Name of Competitor . . . F. Hogget
Name of Entry . . . Pig

The simple truth.

Shepherds usually give their dogs short names, like Gyp or Moss – it's so much quicker and easier than shouting 'Bartholomew!' or 'Wilhelmina!' – and though someone might say '"Pig"? That's a funny name,' no one in their wildest dreams would guess that simple truth.

The two weeks before the Grand Challenge Trials were two weeks of concentrated activity. Apart from Mrs Hogget who as usual was busy with household duties, everyone now knew what was going on. To begin with, Hogget altered the practice course, cutting out all the frills like the plank bridge over the stream, and building a new course as like as possible to what he thought they might face on the day.

As soon as Fly saw this, she became convinced that the plan which she had suspected was actually going to be put into operation, and she told the sheep, with whom she was now on speaking terms.

Every night of course she and Babe talked endlessly about the coming challenge before they settled to sleep (in the stables still, though the Hoggets would have been perfectly happy for Babe to sleep in the house, so well-mannered was he).

Thoughtful as ever, Babe was anxious, not about his own abilities but about his foster-mother's feelings. He felt certain she would have given her dog-teeth to compete in the National Trials, the dream of every sheep-dog, yet she must sit and watch him.

'Are you *sure* you don't mind, Mum?' he asked.

Fly's reply was as practical as ever.

'Listen, Babe,' she said. 'First of all it wouldn't matter whether I minded or not. The boss is going to run you, no doubt of it. Second, I'm too old and too fat, and anyway I was only ever good enough for small local competitions. And lastly, I'll be the happiest collie in the world if you win. And you can win.'

'D'you really think so?'

'I'm sure of it,' said Fly firmly, but all the same she was anxious too – about one thing.

She knew that the sheep-pig, speedy as he now was, would still be much slower than the dogs, especially on the outrun; but equally she was confident that he could make this up by the promptness with which the sheep obeyed his requests. Here, at home, they shot through gaps or round obstacles as quick as a flash, never putting a foot wrong; the ones to be shed nipped out of the ring like lightning; and at the final penning, they popped in the instant that the boss opened the gate. But that was here, at home. What would strange sheep do? How would they react to Babe? Would he be able to communicate with them, in time, for there would be none to waste?

She determined to ask the flock, and one evening, when Babe and the boss were watching television, she trotted off up the hill. Since that first time when she had been forced to speak civilly to them, they no longer cried 'Wolf!' at her, and now they gathered around attentively at her first words, words that were carefully polite.

'Good evening,' said Fly. 'I wonder if you could

be kind enough to help me? I've a little problem,' and she explained it, speaking slowly and carefully (for sheep are stupid, she said to herself: nobody will ever persuade me otherwise).

'You see what I mean?' she finished. 'There they'll be, these strange sheep, and I'm sure they'll do what he tells them . . . asks them, I mean . . . eventually, but it'll all take time, explaining things. The last creature they'll be expecting to see is a pig, and they might just bolt at the sight of him, before he even gets a chance to speak to them.'

'Password,' said several voices.

'What do you mean?' Fly said.

'Password, password, pa-a-a-a-assword!' said many voices now, speaking slowly and carefully (for wolves are stupid, they said to themselves: nobody will ever persuade us otherwise).

'What our Babe's got to do,' said one, 'is to larn what all of us larned when we was little lambs.'

''Tis a saying, see,' said another, 'as lambs do larn at their mothers' hocks.'

'And then wherever we do go . . .'

'. . . to ma-a-a-a-arket . . .'

'. . . or to another fa-a-a-a-arm . . .'

'. . . we won't never come to no ha-a-a-a-arm . . .'

'. . . so long as we do say the pa-a-a-assword!'

'And if our Babe do say it to they . . .'

'. . . why then, they won't never run away!'

Fly felt her patience slipping, but she controlled herself, knowing how important this information could be.

'Please,' she said quietly, 'please will you tell me the password?'

For a long moment the flock stood silent, the only movement a turning of heads as they looked at one another. Fly could sense that they were nerving themselves to tell this age-old secret, to give away – to a wolf, of all things – this treasured countersign.

Then ''Tis for Babe,' someone said, ''tis for his sa-a-a-ake.'

'Ah!' they all said softly. 'A-a-a-a-a-a-ah!' and
then with one voice they began to intone:
'I may be ewe, I may be ram,
I may be mutton, may be lamb,
But on the hoof or on the hook,
I bain't so stupid as I look.'

Then by general consent they began to move
away, grazing as they went.

'Is that it?' called Fly after them. 'Is that the password?' and the murmur came back 'A-a-a-a-a-a-a-a-a-a-ar!'

'But what does it all mean, Mum?' said Babe that night when she told him. 'All that stuff about "I may be you" and other words I don't understand. It doesn't make sense to me.'

'That doesn't matter, dear,' said Fly. 'You just get it off by heart. It may make all the difference on the day.'

Eleven
'Today Is the Day'

The day, when it dawned, was just that little bit too bright.

On the opposite side of the valley the trees and houses and haystacks stood out clearly against the background in that three-dimensional way that means rain later.

Farmer Hogget came out and sniffed the air and looked around. Then he went inside again to fetch waterproof clothing.

Fly knew, the moment that she set eyes on the

boss, that this was the day. Dogs have lived so long with humans that they know what's going to happen, sometimes even before their owners do. She woke Babe.

'Today,' she said.

'Today what, Mum?' said Babe sleepily.

'Today is the day of the Grand Challenge Sheep Dog Trials,' said Fly proudly. 'Which you, dear,' she added in a confident voice, 'are going to win!' With a bit of luck, she thought, and tenderly she licked the end of his snout.

She looked critically at the rest of him, anxious as any mum that her child should be well turned out if it is to appear in public.

'Oh Babe!' she said. 'Your coat's in an awful mess. What have you been doing with yourself? You look just as though you've been wallowing in the duck-pond.'

'Yes.'

'You mean you have?'

'Yes, Mum.'

Fly was on the point of saying that puppies

don't do such things, when she remembered that he was, after all, a pig.

'Well, I don't know about Large White,' she said. 'You've certainly grown enormous but it's anyone's guess what colour you are under all that muck. Whatever's to be done?'

Immediately her question was answered.

'Come, Pig,' said Hogget's voice from the yard, and when they came out of the stables, there stood the farmer with hosepipe and scrubbing brush and pails of soapy water.

Half an hour later, when a beautifully clean shining Babe stood happily dripping while Hogget brushed out the tassel of his tight-curled tail till it looked like candy-floss, Mrs Hogget stuck her head out of the kitchen window.

'Breakfast's ready,' she called, 'but what in the world bist doing with thik pig, taking him to a pig show or summat, I thought you was going to drive up and watch the Trials today, anybody'd think you was going to enter 'e in them the way you've got un done up, only he wouldn't be a sheep-dog, he'd be a sheep-pig wouldn't 'e, tee hee, whoever heard of such a thing, I must be daft though it's you that's daft really, carrying him about in the poor old Land Rover the size he is now, the bottom'll fall out, I shouldn't wonder, you ain't surely going to drive all that way with him in the back just so's he can watch?'

'No,' said Farmer Hogget.

Mrs Hogget considered this answer for a moment with her mouth open, while raising and lowering her eyebrows, shaking her head, and drumming on the window-sill with her finger-tips. Then she closed her mouth and the window.

After breakfast she came out to see them off. Fly was sitting in the passenger seat, Babe was comfortable in a thick bed of clean straw in the back, of which he now took up the whole space.

Mrs Hogget walked round the Land Rover, giving out farewell pats.

'Good boy,' she said to Babe, and 'Good girl,' to Fly. And to Hogget, 'Goodbye and have you got your sandwiches and your thermos of coffee and your raincoat, looks as if it might rain, thought I felt a spot just now though I suppose it might be different where you'm going seeing as it's a hundred miles away, that reminds me have you got enough petrol or if not enough money to get some if you haven't if you do see what I do mean, drive carefully, see you later.'

'Two o'clock,' said Hogget. And before his wife had time to say anything, added, 'On the telly. Live,' and put the Land Rover into gear and drove away.

When Mrs Hogget switched the television on at two o'clock, the first thing in the picture that she noticed was that it was raining hard. She dashed outside to fetch her washing in, saw that the sun was shining, remembered it wasn't washing-day anyway, and came back to find the cameras showing the lay-out of the course. First there was a shot of a huge pillar of stone, the height of a man, standing upright in the ground.

'Here,' said the voice of the commentator, 'is where each handler will stand, and from here

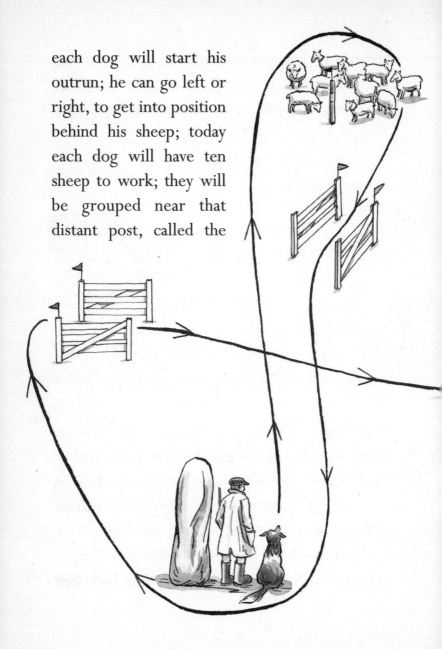

each dog will start his
outrun; he can go left or
right, to get into position
behind his sheep; today
each dog will have ten
sheep to work; they will
be grouped near that
distant post, called the

Holding Post,' (all the time the cameras followed his explanations), 'and then he must fetch his sheep, through the Fetch Gates, all the way back

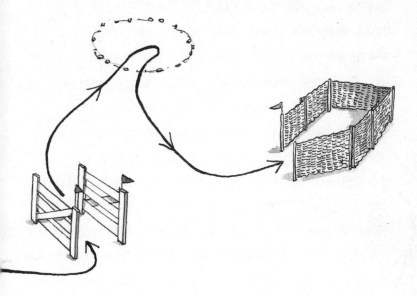

to the Handler's Post, and round it; then the dog drives the sheep away – to the left as we look at it – through the Drive Away Gates, turns them right again and straight across the line of his fetch, through the Cross Drive Gates, and right again to the Shedding Ring, and when he's shed his sheep and collected them again, then finally he must pen them here.'

'Mouthy old thing!' said Mrs Hogget, turning the sound off. 'Some folk never know how to hold their tongues, keeping on and on about them silly gates, why don't 'e show us a picture of the spectators, might catch a glimpse of Hogget and Fly, you never knows, though not the pig, I hopes, he's surely not daft enough to walk about with the pig, can't see why he wanted to take un all that way just to lie in the back of the Land Rover, he'd have done better to leave un here and let un sit and watch it on the telly in comfort which is more than some of us have got time for, I got work to do,' and she stumped off into the kitchen, shaking her head madly.

On the silent screen the first handler walked out and took up his position beside the great sarsen-stone, his dog standing by him, tense and eager in the pouring rain.

Twelve
'That'll Do'

Hundreds of thousands of pairs of eyes watched that first dog, but none more keenly than those of Hogget, Fly and Babe.

The car-park was a big sloping field overlooking the course, and the farmer had driven the Land Rover to the topmost corner, well away from other cars. From inside it, the three so different faces watched intently.

Conditions, Hogget could see immediately, were very difficult. In addition to the driving rain, which made the going slippery and the sheep more obstinate than usual, there was quite a strong wind blowing almost directly from the Holding Post back towards the handler, and the dog was finding it hard to hear commands.

The more anxious the dog was, the more the sheep tried to break from him, and thus the angrier he became. It was a vicious circle, and when at last the ten sheep were penned and the handler pulled the gate shut and cried 'That'll do!' no one was surprised that they had scored no more than seventy points out of a possible hundred.

So it went on. Man after man came to stand beside the great sarsen-stone, men from the North and from the West, from Scotland, and Wales, and Ireland, with dogs and bitches, large and small, rough-coated and smooth, black-and-white or grey or brown or blue merle. Some fared better than others of course, were steadier on their sheep or had steadier sheep to deal with. But still, as Farmer Hogget's turn drew near (as luck would have it, he was last to go), there was no score higher than eighty-five.

At home Mrs Hogget chanced to turn the sound of the television back up in time to hear the commentator confirm this.

'One more to go,' he said, 'and the target to beat is eighty-five points, set by Mr Jones from Wales and his dog Bryn, a very creditable total considering the appalling weather conditions we have up here today. It's very difficult to see that score being beaten, but here comes the last competitor to try and do just that,' and suddenly there appeared on the screen before Mrs Hogget's astonished eyes the tall long-striding figure of her husband, walking out towards the great stone with tubby old Fly at his heels.

'This is Mr Hogget with Pig,' said the commentator. 'A bit of a strange name that, but then I must say his

dog's rather on the fat side . . . hullo, he's sending
the dog back . . . what on earth? . . . oh, good
heavens! . . . Will you look at that!'

And as Mrs Hogget and hundreds of thousands
of other viewers looked, they saw Fly go trotting
back towards the car-park.

And from it, cantering through the never-ending rain, came the long, lean, beautifully clean figure of a Large White pig.

Straight to Hogget's side ran Babe, and stood like a statue, his great ears fanned, his little eyes fixed upon the distant sheep.

At home, Mrs Hogget's mouth opened wide, but for once no sound came from it.

On the course, there was a moment of stunned silence and then a great burst of noise.

On the screen, the cameras showed every aspect of the amazing scene – the spectators pointing, gaping, grinning; the red-faced judges hastily conferring; Hogget and Babe waiting patiently; and finally the commentator.

'This is really quite ridiculous,' he said with a shamefaced smile, 'but in point of fact there seems to be nothing in the rule book that says that only sheep-dogs may compete. So it looks as though the judges are bound to allow Mr Hogget to run this, er, sheep-pig I suppose we'll have to call it, ha, ha! One look at it, and the sheep will disappear into the next county without a doubt! Still, we might as well end the day with a good laugh!'

And indeed at that moment a great gale of laughter arose, as Hogget, receiving a most unwilling nod from the judges, said quietly, 'Away to me, Pig,' and Babe began his outrun to the right.

How they roared at the mere sight of him running (though many noticed how fast he went), and at the purely crazy thought of a pig herding sheep, and especially at the way he squealed and squealed at the top of his voice, in foolish excitement they supposed.

But though he was excited, tremendously excited at the thrill of actually competing in the Grand Challenge Sheep Dog Trials, Babe was nobody's fool. He was yelling out the password: 'I may be ewe, I may be ram, I may be mutton, may be lamb, but on the hoof or on the hook, I bain't so stupid as I look,' he hollered as he ran.

This was the danger point – before he'd met his sheep – and again and again he repeated the magic words, shouting above the noise of wind and rain, his eyes fixed on the ten sheep by the Holding Post. Their eyes were just as fixed on him, eyes that bulged at the sight of this great strange animal approaching, but they held steady, and the now distant crowd fell suddenly silent as they saw the pig take up a perfect position behind his sheep, and heard the astonished judges award ten points for a faultless outrun.

Just for luck, in case they hadn't believed their ears, Babe gave the password one last time. '. . . I bain't so stupid as I look,' he panted, 'and a very good afternoon to you all, and I do apologize for having to ask you to work in this miserable weather, I hope you'll forgive me?'

At once, as he had hoped, there was a positive babble of voices.

'Fancy him knowing the pa-a-a-a-a-assword!'

'What lovely ma-a-a-a-anners!'

'Not like they na-a-a-a-asty wolves!'

'What d'you want us to do, young ma-a-a-a-aster?'

Quickly, for he was conscious that time was ticking away, Babe, first asking politely for their attention, outlined the course to them.

'And I would be really most awfully grateful,' he said, 'if you would all bear these points in mind. Keep tightly together, go at a good steady pace, not too fast, not too slow, and walk exactly through the middle of each of the three gates, if

you'd be good
enough. The moment I
enter the shedding-ring,
would the four of you who are wearing collars
(how nice they look, by the way) please walk out
of it. And then if you'd all kindly go straight into
the final pen, I should be so much obliged.'

All this talk took quite a time, and the crowd
and the judges and Mrs Hogget and her hundreds
of thousands of fellow viewers began to feel that
nothing else was going to happen, that the sheep
were never going to move, that the whole thing
was a stupid farce, a silly joke that had fallen flat.

Only Hogget, standing silent in the rain beside the sarsen-stone, had complete confidence in the skills of the sheep-pig.

And suddenly the miracle began to happen.

Marching two by two, as steady as guardsmen on parade, the ten sheep set off for the Fetch Gates, Babe a few paces behind them, silent, powerful, confident. Straight as a die they went towards the distant Hogget, straight between the exact centre of the Fetch Gates, without a moment's hesitation, without deviating an inch from their unswerving course. Hogget said nothing, made no sign, gave no whistle, did not move as the sheep rounded him so closely as almost to brush his boots, and, the Fetch completed, set off for the Drive Away Gates.

Once again, their pace never changing, looking neither to left nor to right, keeping so tight a formation that you could have dropped a big tablecloth over the lot, they passed through the precise middle of the Drive Away Gates, and turned as one animal to face the Cross Drive Gates.

It was just the same here. The sheep passed through perfectly and wheeled for the Shedding Ring, while all the time the judges' scorecards showed maximum points and the crowd watched in a kind of hypnotized hush, whispering to one another for fear of breaking the spell.

'He's not put a foot wrong!'

'Bang through the middle of every gate.'

'Lovely steady pace.'

'And the handler, he's not said a word, not even moved, just stood there leaning on his stick.'

'Ah, but he'll have to move now – you're never going to tell me that pig can shed four sheep out of the ten on his own!'

The Shedding Ring was a circle perhaps forty yards in diameter, marked out by little heaps of sawdust, and into it the sheep walked, still calm, still collected, and stood waiting.

Outside the circle Babe waited, his eyes on Hogget.

The crowd waited.

Mrs Hogget waited.

Hundreds of thousands of viewers waited.

Then, just as it seemed nothing more would happen, that the man had somehow lost control of the sheep-pig, that the sheep-pig had lost interest in his sheep, Farmer Hogget raised his stick and with it gave one sharp tap upon the great sarsen-stone, a tap that sounded like a pistol-shot in the tense atmosphere.

And at this signal Babe walked gently into the circle and up to his sheep.

'Beautifully done,' he said to them quietly. 'I can't tell you how grateful I am to you all. Now, if the four ladies with collars would kindly walk out of the ring when I give a grunt, I should be so much obliged. Then if you would all be good enough to wait until my boss has walked across to the final collecting pen over there and opened its gate, all that remains for you to do is to pop in. Would you do that? Please?'

'A-a-a-a-a-a-ar,' they said softly, and as Babe gave one deep grunt the four collared sheep detached themselves from their companions and calmly, unhurriedly, walked out of the Shedding Ring.

Unmoving, held by the magic of the moment, the crowd watched with no sound but a great sigh of amazement. No one could quite believe his eyes. No one seemed to notice that the wind had dropped and the rain had stopped. No one was surprised when a single shaft of sunshine came suddenly through a hole in the grey clouds and shone full upon the great sarsen-stone.

Slowly, with his long strides, Hogget left it and walked to the little enclosure of hurdles, the final test of his shepherding. He opened its gate and stood, silent still, while the shed animals walked back into the ring to rejoin the rest.

Then he nodded once at Babe, no more, and steadily, smartly, straightly, the ten sheep, with the sheep-pig at their heels, marched into the final pen, and Hogget closed the gate.

As he dropped the loop of rope over the hurdle stake, everyone could see the judges' marks.

A hundred out of a hundred, the perfect performance, never before matched by man and dog in the whole history of sheep-dog trials, but now achieved by man and pig, and everyone went mad!

At home Mrs Hogget erupted, like a volcano, into a great lava-flow of words, pouring them out towards the two figures held by the camera, as though they were actually inside that box in the corner of her sitting-room, cheering them, praising them, congratulating first one and then the other, telling them how proud she was, to hurry home, not to be late for supper, it was shepherd's pie.

As for the crowd of spectators at the Grand Challenge Sheep Dog Trials they shouted and yelled and waved their arms and jumped about, while the astonished judges scratched their heads and the amazed competitors shook theirs in wondering disbelief.

'Marvellous! Ma-a-a-a-a-a-arvellous!' bleated the ten penned sheep. And from the back of an ancient Land Rover at the top of the car-park a tubby old black-and-white collie bitch, her plumed tail wagging wildly, barked and barked and barked for joy.

In all the hubbub of noise and excitement, two figures still stood silently side by side.

Then Hogget bent, and gently scratching Babe between his great ears, uttered those words that every handler always says to his working companion when the job is finally done.

Perhaps no one else heard the words, but there was no doubting the truth of them.

'That'll do,' said Farmer Hogget to his sheep-pig. 'That'll do.'

A whole barnyard of books!

If you loved *The Sheep-Pig*, here are just a few of the other titles by Dick King-Smith…

A golden goose! There's no such thing! Oh yes, there is, and she's living on Farmer Skint's farm.He was a poor unfortunate man but now the golden goose has brought him good luck and happiness. But what will happen if other people find out about his golden bird?

When Babe, the little orphaned piglet, is won at a fair by Farmer Hogget, he is adopted by Fly, the kind-hearted sheep-dog. Babe is determined to learn everything he can from Fly. He knows he can't be a sheep-dog. But maybe, just maybe, he might be a sheep-pig.

The story of Max, the hedgehog
who becomes a hodgeheg, who
becomes a hero!

Max's family dreams of reaching
the Park. But no one has ever found
a safe way of crossing the very
busy road. Can Max really solve the
problem?

Henry the Great Dane is invisible.
Invisible, that is, to everyone except
Janie – and old Mrs Garrow who lives
in the end cottage. Janie loves Henry,
but will she ever have a real dog? And
how does Mrs Garrow know what's
going to happen?

Find out more about Dick King-Smith, his
other titles and more fantastic Puffin authors
by clicking on **www.puffin.co.uk**

**Winner of the
Guardian Children's Fiction Prize**

Here's what the judges had to say about

The Sheep-Pig

★ 'Perfect'   ★ 'Thrilling'

★ 'Funny'

★ 'The Best'

★ 'Charmer'

★ 'Suspense'

★ 'Breathless'

★ 'Delight'